Tarantula Spiders

by Claire Archer

ABDO SPIDERS Kids

Visit us at www.abdopublishing.com

Published by Abdo Kids, a division of ABDO, PO Box 398166, Minneapolis, Minnesota 55439.

Copyright © 2015 by Abdo Consulting Group, Inc. International copyrights reserved in all countries. No part of this book may be reproduced in any form without written permission from the publisher.

Printed in the United States of America, North Mankato, Minnesota.

032014

092014

PRINTED ON RECYCLED PAPER

Photo Credits: Shutterstock, Thinkstock

Production Contributors: Teddy Borth, Jennie Forsberg, Grace Hansen

Design Contributors: Dorothy Toth, Laura Rask

Library of Congress Control Number: 2013952994
Cataloging-in-Publication Data
Archer, Claire.
 Tarantula spiders / Claire Archer.
  p. cm. -- (Spiders)
ISBN 978-1-62970-074-8 (lib. bdg.)
Includes bibliographical references and index.
1. Tarantula spiders--Juvenile literature.   I. Title.
595.4--dc23
 2013952994

Table of Contents

Tarantulas 4

Food 14

Baby Tarantulas 20

More Facts 22

Glossary 23

Index 24

Abdo Kids Code. 24

Tarantulas

Tarantulas can be found in many places around the world. They mainly live in dry deserts and grasslands.

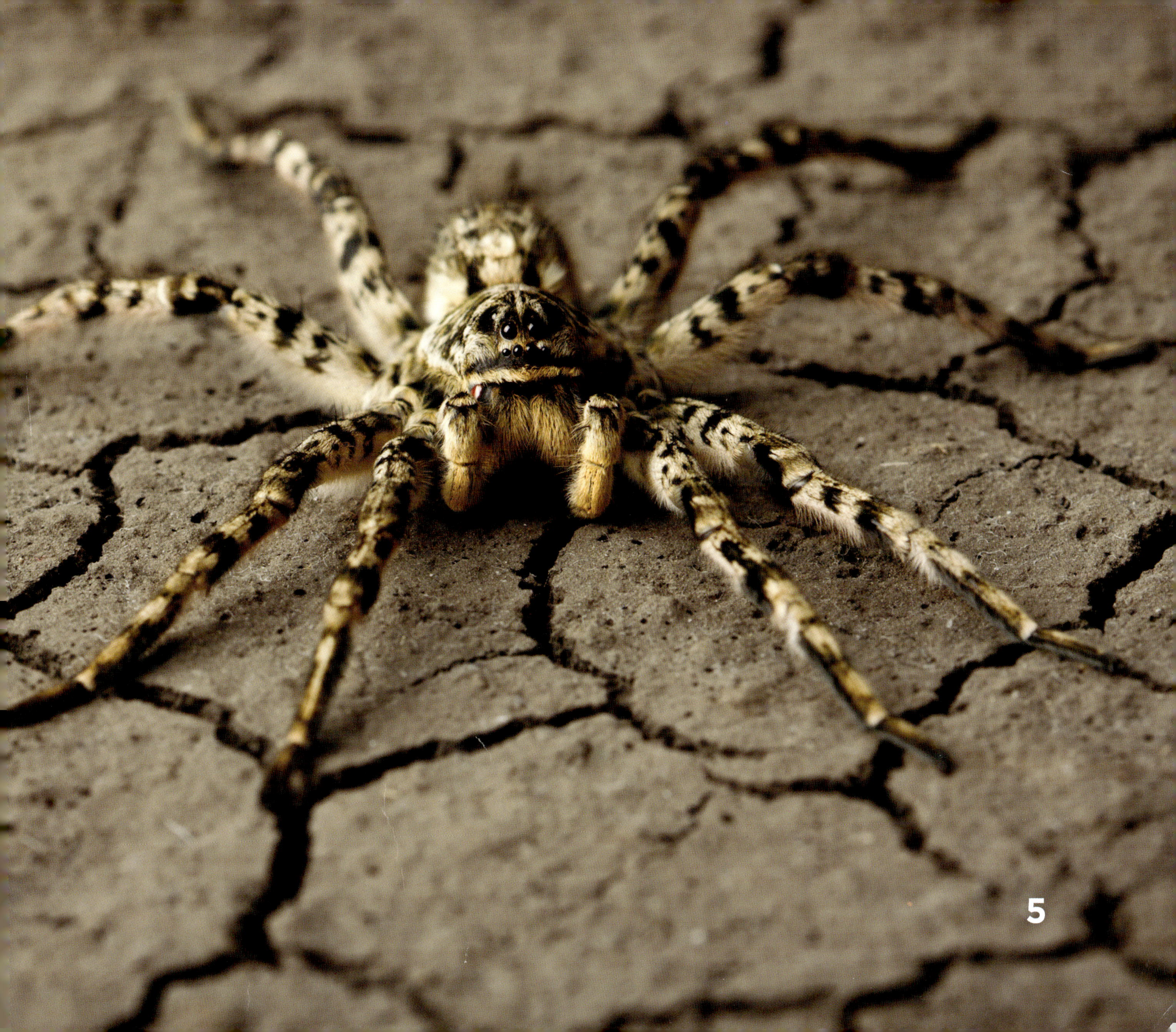

Some tarantulas live in **burrows**. Others live in trees or under rocks and leaves.

7

Most tarantulas are black or brown. Some can be very colorful.

9

Tarantulas are hairy spiders. Even their eight legs are covered with hair.

11

Tarantulas come in all sizes. Some are tiny. Some can be as big as a dinner plate!

13

Food

When hunting, a tarantula will hide and wait for its prey. Then it pounces on its prey.

15

The tarantula bites its **prey**.

Then it injects **venom** that **paralyzes** its prey.

17

Tarantulas eat many animals. They like insects and other spiders. They like mice and birds too.

19

Baby Tarantulas

Female tarantulas lay several hundred eggs at a time. When they hatch, the baby spiders are called spiderlings.

21

More Facts

- Tarantulas that live in **burrows** dig them with their fangs. Some steal other tarantula's homes!

- The tarantula's worst predator is the spider-wasp.

- Some people have pet tarantulas!

Glossary

burrow - an animal's underground home.

paralyze - to cause a loss of motion or feeling in a part of the body.

prey - an animal hunted or killed by a predator for food.

spiderling – a baby spider.

venom - a poison made by some animals and insects. It usually enters a victim through a bite or a sting.

Index

baby tarantulas 20

burrow 6

color 8

desert 4

eggs 20

food 18

grassland 4

habitat 4

hair 10

hunting 14

legs 10

prey 14, 16

size 12

venom 16

abdokids.com

Use this code to log on to abdokids.com and access crafts, games, videos and more!

Abdo Kids Code: **STK0748**